THIS WALKER BOOK BELONGS TO:

To Denise, for all her help with this book

First published 2004 by Walker Books Ltd, 87 Vauxhall Walk, London SE11 5HJ

19 20

© 2004 Anthony Browne

The right of Anthony Browne to be identified as author/illustrator of this work
has been asserted by him in accordance with the Copyright, Designs and Patents Act 1988

This book has been typeset in Poliphilus

Printed in China

British Library Cataloguing in Publication Data: a catalogue record for this book is available from the British Library

ISBN 978-1-84428-559-4

www.walker.co.uk

Into the Forest

Anthony Browne

WALKER BOOKS
AND SUBSIDIARIES
LONDON · BOSTON · SYDNEY · AUCKLAND

One night I was woken up by a terrible sound.

The next morning all was quiet. Dad wasn't there. I asked Mum when he was coming back but she didn't seem to know.

I missed Dad.

The next day Mum asked me to take a cake to Grandma,
who was poorly. I love Grandma. She always tells me
such fantastic stories.

There are two ways to get to Grandma's house: the long way
round, which takes ages, or the short way through the forest.

"Don't go into the forest," said Mum. "Go the long way round."

But that day, for the first time, I chose the quick way. I wanted to be home in case Dad came back.

After a short while I saw a boy.

"Do you want to buy a nice milky moo-cow?" he asked.

"No," I said. (Why would I want a cow?)

"I'll swap it for that sweet fruity-cake in your basket," he said.

"No, it's for my poorly grandma," I said, and walked on.

"*I'm* poorly," I heard him saying, "*I'm* poorly…"

As I went further into the forest I met a girl with golden hair.

"What a sweet little basket," she said. "What's in it?"

"A cake for my grandma. She's poorly."

"*I'd* like a lovely cake like that," she said.

I walked on and could hear her saying, "But it's a lovely little cake, *I'd* like one like that…"

The forest was becoming darker and colder, and I saw two other children huddling by a fire.

"Have you seen our dad and mum?" the boy asked.

"No, have you lost them?"

"They're cutting wood in the forest somewhere," said the girl, "but I wish they'd come back."

As I walked on I could hear the dreadful sound of the girl crying, but what could I do?

I was getting very cold and wished that I'd brought a coat.
Suddenly I saw one. It was nice and warm, but as soon as I put
it on I began to feel scared. I felt that something was following me.
I remembered a story that Grandma used to tell me about a bad wolf.
I started to run, but I couldn't find the path. I ran and ran, deeper
into the forest, but I was lost. Where was Grandma's house?

At last – there it was!

I knocked on the door and a voice called out, "Who's there?" But it didn't really sound like Grandma's voice.

"It's me. I've brought a cake from Mum."

I pushed the door open a little.

"Come in, dear," the strange voice called.

I was terrified. I slowly crept in.

There in Grandma's bed was …

Grandma!

"Come here, love," she sniffed. "How are you?"

"I'm all right now," I said.

Then, I heard a noise behind me and turned round...

DAD!

I told them everything that had happened. We all had a hot drink and I ate two pieces of Mum's delicious cake. Then we said goodbye to Grandma, who was feeling much better.

When we got home I pushed open the door.

"Who's there?" a voice called.

"It's only us," we said.

And Mum came out, smiling.

Anthony Browne

Winner of multiple awards – including the prestigious Kate Greenaway Medal,
the much coveted Hans Christian Andersen Award and the Children's Laureate 2009–2011 –
Anthony is one of the most celebrated author–illustrators of his generation. Renowned for his
unique style, his work is loved around the world.

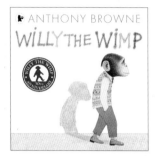

ISBN 978-1-4063-5641-0

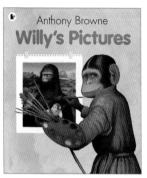

ISBN 978-1-4063-1356-7

ISBN 978-1-4063-1357-4

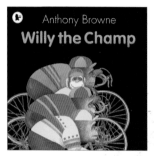

ISBN 978-1-4063-1873-9

ISBN 978-1-4063-0576-0

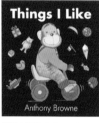

ISBN 978-0-7445-9858-2

ISBN 978-1-4063-1852-4

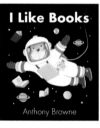

ISBN 978-0-7445-9857-5

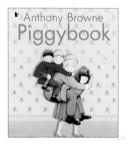

ISBN 978-1-4063-1328-4

ISBN 978-1-4063-5233-7

ISBN 978-1-4063-1930-9

ISBN 978-1-4063-1339-0

ISBN 978-1-4063-1329-1

Available from all good booksellers

www.walker.co.uk